Riddle of the Rusty Horseshoe

by Penumbra Quill

Little, Brown and Company
New York Boston

Little, Brown and Company
Hachette Book Group
1290 Avenue of the Americas, New York, NY 10104
Visit us at LBYR.com
mylittlepony.com

First Edition: October 2017

Little, Brown and Company is a division of Hachette Book Group, Inc. The Little, Brown name and logo are trademarks of Hachette Book Group, Inc.

The publisher is not responsible for websites (or their content) that are not owned by the publisher.

Library of Congress Control Number 2017946350

ISBNs: 978-0-316-55737-5 (pbk.), 978-0-316-55739-9 (ebook)

Printed in the United States of America

LSC-C

10 9 8 7 6 5 4 3 2 1

PROLOGUE

The Pony moved through the Everfree Forest, making no noise at all, almost as if they were part of the shadows themselves. They passed the ridiculously cheerful nest of the bogle and groaned in disgust. Thanks to those annoyingly resourceful Cutie Mark Crusaders, the bogle now had a taste for bright, pretty fabrics and shiny objects. How embarrassing! The Pony slipped past the Poison Joke Tree and traveled deeper into the darkness, finally arriving at their intended destination.

The Pony stood at the edge of a clearing. This was as close as they could get to the Livewood. No amount of magic would keep the twisting vines and branches from noticing them. Just then, a deep growl caught The Pony's attention. Four Timberwolves glared at The Pony from beyond the writhing trees. The Livewood was their home, and what The Pony desired was theirs to guard.

The Pony could feel the magic pouring out of the Livewood and shivered with the need to find a way in. The Pony knew what was inside, just waiting to be taken. But first The Pony had to find a way to keep the Cutie Mark Crusaders from getting any closer to the secrets that would lead them here.

CHAPTER ONE

"Be careful!" Sweetie Belle called to Scootaloo. "If you fall, the lava is going to burn you to a crisp!"

"I can't make it!" Scootaloo said, looking down nervously.

"You got this, Scootaloo!" Apple Bloom said. Scootaloo stared ahead at the giant chasm. Apple Bloom and Sweetie Belle stood anxiously on the other side. She took a deep breath and leaped toward them! Wings flapping frantically, she sailed through the air...but not far enough.

"No!" Scootaloo called, reaching out with a hoof as she fell to her doom.

"I don't get it," Lilymoon said, standing off to the side watching the life-or-death struggle unfold in front of her. Apple Bloom and Sweetie Belle stood on top of the bookcase in Lilymoon's bedroom. Scootaloo was on the ground between the bed and the bookcase in the throes of agony. She stopped writhing and looked over at Lilymoon, rolling her eyes.

"What's to get?" Scootaloo asked, hopping up. "The floor is lava. Anything that's not the floor is safe. If you touch the floor, you're out."

Lilymoon looked dubiously at the Crusaders. "And this is really what other fillies do at sleepovers?" she asked.

"Yeah. The good ones, anyway," Scootaloo said confidently.

"I still don't get it," Lilymoon said again.

"It's just *fun!*" Scootaloo said. "You know, fun? That thing ponies do when they aren't being attacked by crazy monsters?" When it came to battling a bogle or tracking a Timberwolf, Lilymoon was definitely the kind of pony you wanted on your side. But Scootaloo was realizing that when it came to simply hanging out, Lilymoon had a lot to learn.

"Well, this is your house and your first sleepover," Apple Bloom interjected as she hopped down off the bookcase. "What do you want to do?" When Lilymoon had casually admitted she had never had friends over for a sleepover, Apple Bloom said they had to plan one right away. Between the creepy house and Lilymoon's strange family, Scootaloo wasn't sure spending the night here would have been her first choice for a relaxing evening, but Apple Bloom had insisted.

"I really don't know *what* we should do," Lilymoon admitted after considering for a few seconds.

"Well," Apple Bloom said, "we could play board games, do arts and crafts, tell ghost stories. Whatever we want!" Lately, Apple Bloom and Lilymoon had been spending a *lot* of time together. Scootaloo felt like Apple Bloom had made it her personal mission to show Lilymoon what fun and friendship was all about. And of course, Scootaloo knew Apple Bloom meant well. But she couldn't help noticing that the more focused Apple Bloom was on Lilymoon, the less attention she gave Scootaloo and Sweetie Belle.

"Well, I *do* like spooky things," Lilymoon stated. "I bet I could tell some good ghost stories!"

"Great!" Apple Bloom said. "The spookier, the better!" Scootaloo glanced at Sweetie Belle, who looked less than excited at the prospect of spooky stories told in the bedroom of an already-scary house.

"Is that okay with you, Sweetie Belle?" Scootaloo asked.

"Why wouldn't it be okay with her?" Apple Bloom challenged. Sweetie Belle looked back and forth between her two friends.

"It's fine. Ghost stories sound great." Sweetie Belle was trying to act excited, but Scootaloo knew that even though Sweetie Belle had been very brave as of late, particularly when they were hunting the Timberwolf, she still wasn't the type of pony who liked getting scared for fun. Of course, that was something Apple Bloom would have thought about as well, if she weren't so focused on making sure Lilymoon was having the perfect sleepover.

"Okay, y'all. Let's set the mood," Apple Bloom said as she turned the lights down in the room.

"You sure you're okay with this?" Scootaloo whispered to Sweetie Belle.

"I'll be fine," Sweetie Belle whispered back. "You don't think Lilymoon's story will be that scary, do you?" They both looked over at Lilymoon, who stared at them ominously, her piercing violet eyes shining brightly.

"The story I'm about to tell you is the most terrifying tale I ever heard—" Lilymoon whispered. Sweetie Belle groaned quietly next to Scootaloo.

"Hey, maybe I should go first!"

Scootaloo interrupted. At least she could make sure her story wasn't too scary. In fact, she could tell a ghost story Sweetie Belle already knew! She grabbed a blanket and pulled it around her like a shawl. "The tale of the *Olden Pony*! It was a night *just* like this one—"

"Hey now! Lilymoon wanted to tell her story!" Apple Bloom said, annoyed. "Besides, that story ain't scary. We've *heard* it!"

"*Lilymoon* hasn't heard it," Scootaloo shot back.

"I don't have to go first," Lilymoon said nervously. She was clearly uncomfortable with the arguing. "Who is this Olden Pony?"

"She's older than *anypony* you've ever seen," Scootaloo said. "And she's looking for her rusty horseshoe."

"That's not how the story starts!" Apple Bloom groaned. "*First* there's the young ponies on a date—"

"It's *my* story," Scootaloo said.

"*Your* story? Why? 'Cause it gave you nightmares the first time you heard it?" Apple Bloom shot back. Scootaloo gaped at Apple Bloom. She couldn't believe she had just said that! Nopony aside from the Crusaders and Rainbow Dash knew how much that story had scared her, and Apple Bloom had just blurted it out in front of Lilymoon!

"Maybe we should play a game? Oubliettes and Ogres?" Sweetie Belle said, trying to calm things down.

"You all can do whatever you want to do," Scootaloo said, dropping the "shawl" and walking toward the bedroom door. "I'm going downstairs. I...need a snack."

"Should we all do that?" Lilymoon asked.

"No," Scootaloo said firmly. "I'm fine by myself." Scootaloo hurried out of the room, slamming the door behind her.

CHAPTER TWO

Scootaloo stormed down the dark hallway. She, Sweetie Belle, and Apple Bloom had been best friends for as long as she could remember. The three of them had been through so much together. But ever since Lilymoon and her family had shown up, things seemed to be changing, and Scootaloo didn't like it. It wasn't that she didn't like Lilymoon. If anything, life in Ponyville had been more interesting than ever since Lilymoon's family moved into the house on Horseshoe Hill. But things between Apple Bloom and Scootaloo were different now, and she wasn't sure what to do about it.

Scootaloo jumped as something

creaked in the shadows. She might like Lilymoon, but she didn't feel the same about Lilymoon's house. It always felt like somepony was watching you. Scootaloo looked at the framed pictures on the wall as she walked down the hall. There were no photos of Lilymoon and her sister, Ambermoon, as little fillies, no fun family vacation pictures. Instead, there were photos of strange creatures Scootaloo had never heard of hanging next to maps and old newspaper clippings. It looked more like a museum than a home.

Something creaked again. Closer this time.

"Hello?" Scootaloo whispered. But nopony answered. She rolled her eyes. "Come on, Scootaloo. It's just your imagination," she muttered to herself.

She made her way down the stairs to the first floor. Something howled in the distance outside. Scootaloo trotted over to a window and stared out at the backyard. The house on Horseshoe Hill was closer to the Everfree Forest than any other house in Ponyville. In fact, technically it was *in* the forest, although just barely. Behind the house stood the shadowy hulk of Lilymoon's family's greenhouse, and beyond *that* stretched the dark wilds of the Everfree Forest. Scootaloo gulped as she studied the backyard. Who knew what kinds of creatures were lurking just outside the window? Creatures looking to make a late-night snack of a small pony who was herself looking for a late-night snack....

"What are you doing?" a voice whispered in her ear.

"AHHHHHPLEASEDONTEATME!"
Scootaloo yelled. Startled, she ran as fast
as she could, right out the back door. She
wasn't paying attention to where she was
going; she just wanted to get away from
whatever was behind her. However, she
quickly realized that there could be
something just as dangerous *outside* the
house, which meant she wasn't any safer
than she had been. Moonlight glinting off
smoky green glass caught her eye.

Scootaloo changed direction and
rushed toward the shelter of the
greenhouse. Once inside, she hurried past
the reaching leaves and tangled stems of
the strange flora toward the back of the
greenhouse to find a good hiding spot, and
glanced behind her to see if she was being
followed. She didn't see anypony…or any

other creature. But just as Scootaloo turned to face forward again, she slammed into a huge ceramic pot and fell backward. The pot—and the large feathery plant inside it—wobbled. She reached out to keep it from tipping, but it was too late. The pot crashed over, pouring dirt and the feathery plant onto the floor.

"Scootaloo?" an annoyed voice shouted. "Why are you in my dad's greenhouse in the middle of the night?"

Scootaloo knew that voice. It was Ambermoon, Lilymoon's sister. She and Scootaloo did *not* get along.

CHAPTER THREE

"What do you think you're doing out here?" Ambermoon called from the front of the greenhouse.

Scootaloo looked at the fallen plant. Great! *Another* reason for Ambermoon to get snotty with her. She quickly set the pot upright and scooped a few hoof-fuls of dirt back into it before grabbing the feathery plant and jamming it into the pot. Just then, Ambermoon trotted around a large purple cactus and spotted her. She glared at Scootaloo. So Scootaloo glared back.

"What are you up to?" Ambermoon asked suspiciously. "And why did you run out of the house when I tried to talk to you?"

"You mean when you tried to scare me?" Scootaloo responded angrily. Ambermoon rolled her eyes.

"I just wanted to know why you were sneaking around my house in the middle of the night!" Ambermoon shot back.

"I wasn't *sneaking*. I was going to get a snack," Scootaloo explained.

"So you steal our food, snoop around our house, and don't actually sleep. Is that how a sleepover works?" Ambermoon glanced at the greenery next to her. "Should I make sure you didn't take any plants while you were at it?"

"With an attitude like that, it's no wonder you don't know what happens at a sleepover. Who would want to hang out with you?" Scootaloo trotted past

Ambermoon. "Now, if you'll excuse me, I'm going to the kitchen."

"Me too. To make sure you don't go poking around anywhere else you're not invited."

"Whatever." Scootaloo huffed. They both walked back into the house. Scootaloo studied Ambermoon out of the corner of her eye as they went. It wasn't just that Scootaloo didn't really like her; she also didn't trust her. The Crusaders were pretty sure that Ambermoon was responsible for their recent Timberwolf trouble. At the Schoolhouse, Twist had taken a candy cane from Lilymoon's lunch bag. When she ate it, the candy cane transformed Twist into a werepony! The Crusaders and Lilymoon had to get a spell from Zecora to cure her. Later, they found out that the candy cane had come from Ambermoon's room. Scootaloo could think of a few reasons somepony might have a candy cane that could turn another pony into a monster, and none of them were good. But the Crusaders wanted to wait for more proof before they told Lilymoon their suspicions. Until then, they had agreed to keep an eye out for anything else that seemed odd. Like Ambermoon sneaking around in the middle of the night…

"So," Scootaloo said casually as they entered the kitchen, "why are *you* awake?"

Ambermoon studied the kitchen counter as she answered. "My room is right next to Lilymoon's. You four were keeping me up with all your carrying on."

"Oh," Scootaloo said. They probably

had been pretty loud. "How much did you hear?" Without looking up, Ambermoon arched an eyebrow.

"Enough to know that this 'snack break' is just an excuse to get away from your friends for a while."

Great! So she knew Scootaloo was mad at Apple Bloom. Ambermoon was the *last* pony Scootaloo wanted in her business!

"It's no big deal," Scootaloo said quickly.

"Of course not." Ambermoon sounded annoyed. "You felt left out for the first time in your life. Did you expect me to give you a pep talk?"

"So you just came out here to rub it in?" Scootaloo demanded.

"No!" Ambermoon was quiet for a minute, weighing her options, then she finally said, "I…was just making sure you were okay." Scootaloo was speechless. Why would Ambermoon, who had never been anything but mean to her, care if she was okay?

"Where is it?" a strange voice whispered.

"What was that?" Scootaloo said, looking around the room.

"I said I wanted to make sure you were okay," Ambermoon repeated.

"Not that. The other thing!" Scootaloo ran past Ambermoon and looked down the dark hallway.

"What other thing?" Ambermoon looked around, confused.

"WHERE IS IT?" The voice was raspy. And it was getting louder.

"That!" Scootaloo rushed out of the kitchen toward the foyer, following the noise. It sounded like something she had

heard once before in a dream. But it couldn't be...

"Hey! Wait up!" Ambermoon called after her.

Scootaloo rushed into the foyer and gasped. There, at the top of the stairs, slowly walking toward her, was the Olden Pony from her ghost story! But this was no ghost story; this was a very real pony. And she walked slowly down the very real stairs, muttering to herself in a terrifying low growl.

The Olden Pony looked just like Scootaloo remembered from her nightmares. She was ancient, with knobby knees and flea-bitten flanks. She wore a tattered shawl that was hundreds of moons old. Wisps of white mane stuck out from her bun. Two long hairs grew out of a mole on her wrinkled chin. One red eye squinted shut while the other glowed bright blue. And it was glaring straight at Scootaloo.

She couldn't believe it. The Olden Pony was real.

"Where is my rusty horseshoe?" the Olden Pony moaned.

Scootaloo panicked. She desperately dashed for the front door, shoving past Ambermoon, who had just entered the foyer.

"Scootaloo! Why are you acting so weird?" Scootaloo heard Ambermoon call after her. But she couldn't stop. Her hooves wouldn't let her. She just had to get away from the Olden Pony. She had to get home.

CHAPTER FOUR

The next morning, when Scootaloo opened her eyes and found herself in her own bed, she briefly thought everything had been a dream. She hopped up and headed toward the kitchen. But when she rushed into the hallway, she heard a curdling scream.

"Oh! For Celestia's sake!" an Earth pony exclaimed, picking up the basket of laundry she'd just dropped. "What are you doing here, Scootaloo? I thought you were spending the night up at your new friend's house?" So it hadn't been a dream. Scootaloo *had* gotten in a fight with Apple Bloom and run into a creature right out of her nightmares. Awesome.

"Hey, Aunt Holiday," Scootaloo said sullenly. "I…wasn't feeling good so I came home." Aunt Holiday studied Scootaloo with concern, clearly not buying it. But she didn't pry; Aunt Holiday always let Scootaloo tell her things when she was ready.

"Well, head on into the kitchen. Auntie Lofty's already in there. I'll make you some breakfast in just a second."

Scootaloo nodded and went into the kitchen, where a sturdy Pegasus, Auntie Lofty, was scarfing down a plate of eggs. She looked up at Scootaloo, surprised.

"Hey, slugger! What are you doing here?" Auntie Lofty asked.

"I came home last night! It's not a big deal!" Scootaloo said more forcefully than she intended. Lofty arched an eyebrow. In contrast to Aunt Holiday, *she* never let things rest until she had answers. Aunt Holiday came trotting into the room and kissed Lofty on top of her head.

"Let me make Scootaloo some breakfast first, dear. *Then* you can give her the third degree." Scootaloo sighed. Aunt Holiday was her dad's older sister. Recently, she and Auntie Lofty had started staying with Scootaloo when her parents were away, which was most of the time. Unlike her parents, they were *always* interested in what was going on in her life. Usually it was nice that they cared, but this morning, she wished they would just leave things be. Scootaloo sat down at the kitchen table, where Auntie Lofty eyed her suspiciously. A knock at the door rescued Scootaloo from Lofty's gaze.

"I'll get it!" Scootaloo said, jumping up and rushing to the door. She opened it to find Apple Bloom, Sweetie Belle, Lilymoon, *and* Ambermoon standing there. They all looked at her with varying degrees of worry.

"Oh. Hey, guys," Scootaloo said, not quite sure what to say.

"Hey," Apple Bloom said, equally as uncomfortable. "We just wanted to make sure you were okay. Ambermoon told us you left in a hurry last night." Scootaloo looked at Ambermoon. Why hadn't she told them about the spooky, old pony on the stairs?

"Well, of course I did...I saw the Olden Pony coming down the stairs toward me. What else was I gonna do?" The fillies all glanced at one another, confused.

Ambermoon looked back at Scootaloo. "There wasn't anypony on the stairs. We were in the kitchen, then you ran into the foyer and out of the house," she explained.

"What? No. I saw her!" Scootaloo insisted. "She was right there on the stairs! She was asking about her rusty horseshoe!" Scootaloo couldn't believe Ambermoon was lying!

"Well," Apple Bloom began, "maybe you just thought you saw the Olden Pony after I reminded you of how scared you used to be of her." She looked like she wanted to say more, but Scootaloo didn't give her a chance.

"Can you *please* stop bringing that up?!" Scootaloo said angrily. "I don't need you telling everypony else what a scaredy-pony you think I am!"

"That ain't what I'm sayin'!" Apple Bloom responded.

"You're just saying you don't believe me," Scootaloo said.

"Well, if Ambermoon didn't see anything—" Sweetie Belle began.

"Oh, so *now* you trust Ambermoon?" Scootaloo asked.

"What does *that* mean?" Ambermoon said, looking at the others.

"Nothin'," Apple Bloom said. She turned to Scootaloo. "Okay, so you think you saw something last night."

"I *did* see something last night. The Olden Pony," Scootaloo stated.

"But isn't that just a ghost story?" Lilymoon asked. Scootaloo's wings fluttered in annoyance.

"Look," she said, "I *know* it's a ghost story. I *know* she's not supposed to be real. But I also know what I saw. It *was* her. She

was there. I don't know how, but she was."
She looked at the others. She could tell
they were at a loss for what to say. They
really didn't believe her. She was just going
to have to find a way to prove to them it
was true!

"Thanks for coming by to check on
me," Scootaloo said, then forced a fake
yawn and stretched her hooves. "I think
maybe I just need some rest. I'll catch up
with you later."

"You sure?" Sweetie Belle asked. "We
thought maybe we could all go over to
Sugarcube Corner and—"

"It's okay," Scootaloo said quickly, "I'm
not that hungry. Have fun!" She went
back inside, leaving her confused friends to
stare at one another quizzically on the
doorstep.

CHAPTER FIVE

After a hearty breakfast spent avoiding answering Auntie Lofty's questions, Scootaloo headed into town. If she was going to prove that the Olden Pony was real, she needed more information. For that, she knew *just* who to talk to. Scootaloo felt a little bit better now that she had a plan. She just wished she didn't have to do it alone. She was used to having her friends by her side.

"Doesn't look like you're getting much rest," somepony said. Scootaloo turned. Ambermoon was leaning against a tree. Scootaloo huffed and kept walking. Ambermoon rushed over to walk alongside her.

"You sure seem to like following me,"

Scootaloo said. "Planning to spy some more and then lie to my friends that I'm seeing things?"

"I didn't say you were seeing things. I just said *I* didn't see anything. Because I didn't," Ambermoon explained. "But after talking to you this morning, I realized something must have happened—I just wasn't sure what. And that's what I told your friends." Scootaloo still couldn't believe Ambermoon hadn't seen anything, but there was nopony else around, so she had no reason to lie.

"Yeah? Where are they now?" Scootaloo asked, pretending to be disinterested.

"Sugarcube Corner. Although they all looked pretty bummed to go without you." Scootaloo felt better knowing her friends missed her. If only they believed her, too.

"Why did you stick around?" Scootaloo asked, honestly curious. Ambermoon stared straight ahead, not making eye contact.

"I could tell you were planning something. And I saw how scared you were last night. I felt bad. So I…wanted to help if I could." Scootaloo stopped walking and stared at Ambermoon.

"Okay, *hold* on. Last night you said you wanted to check on me. Now you want to help me. We don't even like each other! Why are you doing this?"

"I can see how much Lilymoon likes hanging out with all of you," Ambermoon explained. "She seems…happier since she met you. It made me think…it might be nice to have a friend. So I'm trying to be friendly." Ambermoon looked at Scootaloo and forced a wide smile. The

weird grin had the opposite effect
Ambermoon was going for, but she seemed
to be sincere. Maybe she wasn't as bad as
Scootaloo had thought she was. Scootaloo
still didn't completely trust her, but…it was
nice having somepony on her side. Even if
it wasn't the pony she was expecting.

"Okay, fine," Scootaloo said. "You can
hang out with me. *For now.* C'mon." She
nudged Ambermoon's shoulder to follow.

"Where are we going?" Ambermoon
asked.

"To get answers about the Olden Pony
story from the most awesome pony in
Equestria. The pony who told me the story
in the first place: Rainbow Dash."

It took a little time, a lot of asking
around, and a ton of side errands, but they
finally found Rainbow Dash flying out of

Rarity's boutique. She was carrying her Wonderbolts uniform and was in a hurry.

"Hey! Rainbow Dash!" Scootaloo called, waving at the blue Pegasus. Rainbow Dash saw her and veered over.

"Hey, Scoot. Hey, Scoot's friend. Can't talk long. I'm in a hurry! Gotta get ready to go to Canterlot for the Royal Flyfest! It's gonna be so *awesome*!"

"Oh *wow*! The Flyfest!" Scootaloo exclaimed. "That sounds *amazing*! What tricks are you planning?" Ambermoon cleared her throat, reminding Scootaloo why they were there. "Oh. Right," Scootaloo said. "Hey, before you go, can I ask you something about the Olden Pony?"

"The what now?" Rainbow Dash frowned.

"You know, that spooky story you told me a long time ago." Scootaloo squinted one eye and hobbled toward Rainbow Dash. "'Who has my rusty horseshoe?' Is there any more to it?" Scootaloo asked.

Rainbow Dash shook her head. "Nope. Long time ago. Spooky night. Some ponies walking through the woods; Olden Pony wants her rusty horseshoe. Boom!" Then she added, "I mean, when I tell it, it *feels* like there's more to the story, because I'm a *really* good storyteller." Rainbow Dash glanced around. "Hey, where're Apple Bloom and Sweetie Belle? Aren't you all attached at the flank?"

"Um." Scootaloo kicked a rock with her hoof. "I…don't wanna talk about it."

"Whoa. Whoa." Rainbow Dash landed next to Scootaloo and Ambermoon.

"I may be in a hurry, but I've always got time when something's wrong with a friend. And something is definitely wrong. What's up?"

"Things have just been weird lately," Scootaloo mumbled.

Rainbow Dash nodded. "I see," she said. "Well, I know *just* how to fix that!"

"You do?" Scootaloo asked.

"Yup! Sometimes friendships can go through ups and downs. But doing something awesome together always helps. Go round up the others. You're all gonna be my special guests tomorrow at the Canterlot Royal Flyfest!"

CHAPTER SIX

The rest of the day was a blur of activity.
Scootaloo and Ambermoon rushed to
Sugarcube Corner to tell the others about
the invitation. Despite the weirdness
between Scootaloo and Apple Bloom,
everypony was beyond excited. A chance
to see the Wonderbolts live was never
something anypony would pass up!

Ambermoon and Lilymoon ran home
to make sure it was okay with their parents
that they tag along, while the Crusaders
ran to the clubhouse where they had a pile
of Rainbow Dash posters ready to go.
(Scootaloo always made sure there were
GO, RAINBOW DASH! and RAINBOW DASH IS
AWESOME! posters for any occasion.)

Nopony brought up what Scootaloo had seen the night before. It still bugged Scootaloo that the others didn't believe her, but until she had proof that what she saw was real, she didn't want to get into another argument with Apple Bloom. Apple Bloom seemed to feel the same way. She kept the conversation focused on the Wonderbolts and how much Lilymoon was going to love watching them fly. Sweetie Belle kept glancing back and forth between Scootaloo and Apple Bloom. She knew things weren't fine, but she didn't seem to know what to do about it, so she just kept smiling and saying, "Yay, Wonderbolts," a lot.

Scootaloo was relieved that she made it through the night without seeing or hearing anything strange, and bright and early the next morning the Crusaders, Lilymoon, and Ambermoon met Rainbow Dash at the train station.

"Come on! Let's go, go, go!" Rainbow Dash said as she hurried them all onto the Friendship Express. "I have to get to Canterlot in time to rehearse!"

"This is so exciting!" Lilymoon said, smiling wider than Scootaloo had ever seen. "I've only ever heard about the Wonderbolts! I can't wait to actually see them!" She sat down next to the window as the train slowly left the station.

"It's gonna be amazin'!" Apple Bloom grinned, sitting down next to her. Sweetie Belle climbed into the seat in front of them. Scootaloo saw that Ambermoon was sitting a bit off to the side by herself. She walked past the open seat next to

Sweetie Belle and sat next to Ambermoon instead. Everypony, including Ambermoon, was surprised.

"I'm glad you could come," Scootaloo said as she settled next to the Unicorn. Ambermoon smiled shyly back.

"Me too," she said. "It took some convincing, but since this is the first thing my sister and I have ever wanted to do together, my parents finally gave in." In front of them, Lilymoon said something and Apple Bloom laughed *loudly*. Scootaloo rolled her eyes, then pointedly laughed even louder.

"Ha-ha-ha! That's hilarious, Ambermoon!" Scootaloo shouted. Apple Bloom, Sweetie Belle, and Lilymoon all turned to look back at them. Ambermoon eyed her strangely.

"What about that was hilarious?" she asked.

"Nothing, I just—" Scootaloo began, but a raspy voice cut her off.

"Where is it?" The voice rose from a growl to a shriek. *"WHERE IS MY RUSTY HORSESHOE?"*

"What was that?" Ambermoon yelped, jumping out of her seat and looking around the train. Scootaloo stared at her.

"You heard it, too?" Scootaloo asked.

"Everypony on the train must have heard that!" Ambermoon replied. They both looked around. Apple Bloom, Lilymoon, and Sweetie Belle were chatting softly. In fact, aside from a few passengers eyeing them curiously, everypony else was sitting quietly.

"That was *her*!" Scootaloo whispered.

"The Olden Pony." Ambermoon looked thoughtful, then glanced around the train.

"Okay. Well, even though I don't see her, I clearly heard her. So it isn't just in your head," she said matter-of-factly.

"I *told* you," Scootaloo replied triumphantly.

"But now we need to figure out what's happening. Let's—"

"Hey, you two!" Sweetie Belle called, waving to them. "Come here for a sec!"

"Maybe she heard it, too!" Scootaloo said, and the two of them joined the others. But Sweetie Belle's happy smile made it clear that this wasn't about anything spooky.

"I just wanted to say I'm really glad Ambermoon and Lilymoon could join us for this trip. Scootaloo *and* Apple Bloom and I are looking forward to *all* of us spending time together." Scootaloo realized what the loud *and* between her name and Apple Bloom's meant. It was about as close as Sweetie Belle was going to get to telling her friends to cut it out and play nice. Scootaloo really wanted to get back to talking to Ambermoon about the Olden Pony, but she appreciated what one of her best friends was trying to do.

"Let's all just have fun today," Sweetie Belle added. "Deal?" she said as she stuck out her hoof. Apple Bloom grinned and did the same.

"Deal," Apple Bloom said.

"Deal," Lilymoon and Ambermoon both said as they stuck their hooves in.

"Deal," Scootaloo said, sticking her hoof in and bumping it with the others.

Maybe Rainbow Dash is right, Scootaloo thought. Maybe all you needed to fix friendship problems was a trip to a Wonderbolts show. Now if only that could solve the Olden Pony problem, too....

CHAPTER SEVEN

"Fillies and gentlecolts! Please put your hooves together forrrrrrrrrrr the—" The announcer barely got out the word *"Wonderbolts!"* before the crowd went wild! Ponies screamed and cheered as the Wonderbolts soared over the stadium into the arena. Celestia had just lowered the sun, and giant lights pointing skyward illuminated the Pegasi's trademark blue-and-gold uniforms as they streaked across the star-filled night.

The seating for the Canterlot Royal Arena was built into the side of a huge cliff for perfect viewing. Hundreds of ponies filled the stands, stomping their hooves with excitement as a crew of Pegasi shifted cloud and rainbow obstacles into place for the Wonderbolts' daring maneuvers. Usually Scootaloo would have been cheering louder than anypony, but with everything going on, she was having trouble focusing.

"*Wow!*" exclaimed Lilymoon.

"*Go, Rainbow Dash!*" Sweetie Belle and Apple Bloom screamed.

Sweetie Belle nudged Scootaloo. "Hey, you okay?" Scootaloo glanced over at Ambermoon. Before the show had started, Ambermoon suggested they tell the others what they had heard on the train. But Scootaloo had insisted they wait until *after* the Wonderbolts' performance. She knew Rainbow Dash loved nothing more than performing for her friends, and she wanted everypony's focus to be on her hero.The mystery stuff could wait until later.

"I'm fine," she lied. Scootaloo looked up at the Wonderbolts flying in formation. She easily spotted Rainbow Dash and smiled. Rainbow Dash always got annoyed with this part of the performance, because she said she had to fly slower than she wanted in order to keep pace with the others. But despite that, she always managed to fly at exactly the right speed. Rainbow Dash, Soarin', Spitfire, and the others were all perfectly in sync. Scootaloo glanced over at Apple Bloom. She realized that not being perfectly in sync with her best friend was bothering her just as much as the problem with the Olden Pony. Apple Bloom glanced over and saw Scootaloo looking at her. She gave a small smile and waved. Scootaloo smiled back. Maybe everything would be—

The Olden Pony's voice cut through the crowd like a knife. *"WHERE IS MY RUSTY HORSESHOE?"*

Scootaloo could feel Ambermoon tense up beside her. But this time, she saw Apple Bloom, Sweetie Belle, and Lilymoon freeze as well!

"Rusty horseshoe?" Sweetie Belle squeaked.

"You heard that?" Scootaloo asked.

Apple Bloom nodded, her eyes wide.

"Not just heard it…" Lilymoon said, pointing at the stairs below their seats.

The Olden Pony was slowly hobbling toward them, her red eye glaring balefully at them.

"I know you have it," she croaked, pointing at them. *"Give it to me!"*

But this time, Scootaloo was ready. Back when she'd still had nightmares about the Olden Pony, there had been one way to stop her. Scootaloo pulled a rusty horseshoe out of her saddlebag and tossed it toward the ancient mare.

"Take it!" Scootaloo cried. The Olden Pony squinted down at the horseshoe. Then she gave Scootaloo a wicked smile.

"That's not going to work this time, dearie." Scootaloo gasped as the Olden Pony kicked the horseshoe away and kept stalking toward them.

"Everypony, stay calm," Ambermoon said, taking charge. "We don't know what she is, but we know she isn't real. She can't hurt us."

Scootaloo glanced at the ponies behind and around them. They were whispering to one another and starting to look at the CMCs and their friends strangely. It was obvious that none of the other audience members could see the Olden Pony. Scootaloo looked back down to the stairs and gulped. The Olden Pony was gone.

"Not real? Can't hurt you?" Stale breath brushed Scootaloo's neck. Dreading what she'd see but knowing she had to look, she slowly turned. The Olden Pony was standing right next to her! The ancient mare reached out her hoof and shoved Scootaloo's shoulder. Scootaloo stumbled backward.

"She can touch us!" Scootaloo yelled. More ponies in the crowd turned to see what was

going on. The Olden Pony cackled, the sound of dead leaves tossed in a winter gale.

"NOW, WHERE IS IT?" the Olden Pony demanded.

"Run!" Apple Bloom yelled. The fillies all scrambled away from the terrifying ancient mare.

"Hey!"

"Watch it!"

"What are you doing?"

Ponies yelled as the Crusaders and the Moon Sisters pushed through the crowd in a panic.

"Wait!" shouted Ambermoon. "Even if we escape, aren't the rest of these ponies in danger?"

"I don't know," Scootaloo admitted. At that, Ambermoon turned and started running up the stairs, in the opposite direction of the exit.

"Where are you goin'?" Apple Bloom called.

"The stands aren't safe! Somepony needs to stop the show!" Ambermoon yelled back.

"Stop the *show*?" Scootaloo yelped. She looked at Apple Bloom and Sweetie Belle, panicked. "We can't stop the show!"

Apple Bloom pointed at the Olden Pony, who was closing in on them, moving surprisingly fast for her apparent age.

"We got bigger problems right now, don'tcha think?" The fillies rushed to the top of the stadium. Ambermoon burst into the announcer's booth, the others right behind her. The announcer pony turned and looked at them in shock.

"Hey! You ponies can't be in here!" he exclaimed.

"We have to stop the show right now," Ambermoon said firmly.

"What? *Why?*" the pony asked.

"*Yes, why?*" The Olden Pony was suddenly standing behind the announcer. He didn't seem to hear her and just kept staring at the fillies. *"Afraid I'm going to scare everypony? Cause them to panic?"* With a wicked smile, she reached out and pulled a lever. All the lights in the stadium turned off, leaving everypony in total darkness.

"What happened?" the announcer yelled. Outside the booth, ponies starting yelling and screaming in confusion and panic. Scootaloo couldn't see anything. All she could hear was the laughter of the Olden Pony echoing in her ears.

CHAPTER EIGHT

"I don't even know where to begin."
Rainbow Dash flew back and forth as the
Friendship Express chugged steadily
toward Ponyville. Scootaloo, Apple Bloom,
Sweetie Belle, Lilymoon, and Ambermoon
sat sullenly in their seats. "What were you
thinking?"

"We told you—" Scootaloo began, but
Rainbow Dash held up a hoof.

"Do *not* mention the Olden Pony. The
ponies in the stands said you started
screaming for no reason, pushed through
the crowd, ran up to the booth, and told
the announcer to stop the show. Nopony
saw *anything* following you."

"I know it sounds crazy. And at first we

didn't see anything, either, but it really was—"

Rainbow Dash held up her other hoof. "No. Olden. Pony," she said through gritted teeth. She shook her head and looked down at Scootaloo. "I'm just really disappointed in all of you. You were my guests. And you ruined the entire event." She turned to leave. Scootaloo rushed over and grabbed her hoof.

"I'm really sorry, Rainbow Dash," Scootaloo said. Rainbow Dash shook her head sadly.

"Let's just deal with this later. I'm going up to the front of the train. When we're back in Ponyville, we're getting your families together and we're having a serious talk." She flew out of the train cabin.

Scootaloo stared out the window as the

sun began to rise. She had never felt worse in her entire life. Rainbow Dash had *never* been this upset with her. *Ever.* Scootaloo could feel tears welling up in her eyes. The fight with Apple Bloom, the Olden Pony, and now ruining the Wonderbolts' show? It was all too much. She buried her face in her hooves. A second later, she felt a hoof on her shoulder. She looked up and saw that it was Apple Bloom.

"I'm sorry," she said.

"Why? It's not your fault I'm a huge disappointment to the greatest pony of all time," Scootaloo said sadly.

"No. I mean, I'm sorry about that, too. But...I'm sorry I didn't believe you. And I'm sorry I was mean to you the other night. If I hadn't said what I said about you bein' scared of that story, you never woulda gone downstairs, and none of this woulda happened. It's all my fault."

Scootaloo let out a long sigh and hugged Apple Bloom. "It's not your fault, and I'm sorry, too," she said. "If I'm being honest, I was just jealous. You and Lilymoon have been spending so much time together that I was just worried you'd forget *our* friendship."

"Oh thank goodness!" Lilymoon said, sounding relieved. Everypony turned to stare at her. She blushed and turned to Scootaloo. "I thought you were mad at me for some reason."

"No!" Scootaloo exclaimed. "You're awesome. Things have just been different lately." Scootaloo looked at Ambermoon.

"But I guess different isn't bad. It's just…
different."

"No matter what else changes, you're
always gonna be one of my best friends,"
Apple Bloom said. "And when you're in
trouble, I'll be there. So next time my best
friend says that she sees a scary, old pony
coming after her, I promise I'm going to
believe her."

"That's good," Sweetie Belle said with
a shaky voice as the train pulled into the
Ponyville train station. "Because as your
other best friend, I want to tell you that
there's a scary, old pony coming after us."
She pointed out the window.

The Olden Pony was waiting for them
at the train station.

CHAPTER NINE

"Thought you fillies could hide from me, did you?" The Olden Pony leered at them, pressing her face against the train window. Sweetie Belle leaped back from it so fast, she knocked over Scootaloo.

"No horseplay please," a passing conductor warned them. Scootaloo watched as he opened the carriage door and passengers exited the train, passing the Olden Pony without a glance.

"It's just like at the Wonderbolts show. Nopony sees her but us," whispered Lilymoon.

"But why? And where did she come from?" Ambermoon frowned.

"And how do we get rid of her?" Sweetie Belle wailed.

"That sounds like a job for the Cutie Mark Crusaders! I call an emergency meeting to order!" Apple Bloom blurted. Despite the spooky situation, Scootaloo had to hold back a laugh. Leave it to Apple Bloom to follow club procedure, even when they were being stalked by a ghost story come to life.

The last pony stepped out onto the train platform. Scootaloo hurled herself against the carriage door and slammed it shut, locking it before the Olden Pony could force her way onboard. Furious, the ancient mare scraped her single shoeless hoof against the glass of the window. It made a horrible grating sound.

"WHERE IS MY RUSTY HORSESHOE?" the Olden Pony groaned.

"Can we have this meeting somewhere else?" Scootaloo asked. The others were happy to agree, and they ran through the train car to the next one down the line.

"Everypony, think," Apple Bloom commanded. "Scootaloo, you were the first one of us to see the Olden Pony. Do you have any idea what you did to make her show up?" Scootaloo had been asking herself the same question ever since the slumber party. Unfortunately, she hadn't come up with any answers. She shook her head.

"You first saw her at our house, right?" Lilymoon asked. "So we should go back there and retrace your steps. Maybe that will give us a clue."

The train car shook with a heavy impact from its roof. The fillies froze and listened as heavy hoof-falls echoed above them. *CLANK CLANK CLANK THUMP! CLANK CLANK CLANK THUMP!* It was the sound of three horseshoes and one hoof. The Olden Pony was on top of the train. She was looking for a way in. And the emergency hatch was just over their heads.

"She can't chase us all if we split up," Scootaloo said. "Ambermoon, you run toward the front of the train. I'll go to the back." Ambermoon nodded.

"I'm coming with you," Apple Bloom told Scootaloo firmly.

"Me too!" Sweetie Belle squeaked.

"Guess that means we get some sister time," Lilymoon told Ambermoon. Scootaloo didn't think they seemed too happy about it. But there wasn't time to discuss that, because just then, the Olden Pony popped open the emergency door above them and squinted down, her red eye rolling in its socket.

"Did you miss me?" She brayed a terrifying laugh and lunged at the fillies.

"Meet us at our house!" Ambermoon yelled as she pushed open the train car door. She dashed off in the direction of the engine, Lilymoon hot on her hocks. Scootaloo, Apple Bloom, and Sweetie Belle jumped on the platform a moment later and raced in the other direction. The

voice of the Olden Pony howled behind
them:

*"You can't run from me! I'll find you
wherever you go!"*

And that was the scariest thought of all.

CHAPTER TEN

The CMCs ran until they reached the bottom of Horseshoe Hill, where they stopped to gasp for breath. Scootaloo wished she had her scooter. No way a three-shoed pony could keep up with them then!

"Is she gone?" Sweetie Belle panted. The Crusaders looked around nervously, but it seemed they had finally lost the Olden Pony. Then Scootaloo had a troubling thought.

"I hope that doesn't mean she's chasing Ambermoon and Lilymoon instead," Scootaloo said.

Apple Bloom looked thoughtful. "When did you become such good friends with Ambermoon?" she asked.

Scootaloo shrugged. "I guess when she started being nice to me. She's actually kind of cool, once you spend time with her."

"Yeah…but do you think you can trust her?" Apple Bloom pressed.

"It *was* her candy cane that turned Twist into a werepony," Sweetie Belle pointed out.

"We don't know that's true." Apple Bloom frowned. Scootaloo started to worry that they were heading toward another disagreement. But then Apple Bloom's expression cleared. "I guess we just don't have all the facts yet. And it wouldn't be right to blame Ambermoon for anythin' until we know the whole story."

"Right," Scootaloo agreed with the tiniest sigh of relief.

Hoofbeats sounded behind them, and the trio spun, startled. But instead of the glare of a single red eye, they found

Lilymoon and Ambermoon.

"I'm *so glad* you're not the Olden Pony!" Sweetie Belle said.

"Um, thanks?" Lilymoon said. "Now, let's get to the house before she *does* show up."

The group climbed the hill to the forbidding home atop it.

"Did you ever think about getting a welcome mat?" Sweetie Belle suggested as they all stepped onto the rickety porch.

"No," Ambermoon and Lilymoon answered in unison.

Scootaloo led her friends inside to the giant staircase beyond the foyer. She pointed a hoof.

"There. That's where I first saw the Olden Pony," she told them.

"So we need to work backward from here," Ambermoon said. "Before you ran in this room, we were in the kitchen."

"Yeah." Scootaloo nodded. "I heard the Olden Pony in there. And before that, we walked across the yard...and before that, I was in the greenhouse, and before *that*—"

"Wait. What were you doing in the greenhouse?" Lilymoon asked with a frown. Scootaloo blushed. Now that she thought about it, admitting she was running away from Ambermoon did sound pretty silly.

"She got lost." Ambermoon smoothly covered for her new friend. "I found her in the greenhouse." Scootaloo shot her a grateful look, then picked up the tale.

"And before that, I was in the kitchen. Which is where I went after I left the sleepover."

"Every part of that story sounds pretty normal, except the greenhouse," Apple Bloom mused.

"I'm not sure anything here is normal," Sweetie Belle murmured, pointing a hoof. The other fillies followed it to see Blue Moon headed toward them, "walking" a pair of bats on tiny leashes.

"Hello, Father," Lilymoon and Ambermoon chorused.

"Hello, hello." Blue Moon grinned back. Scootaloo always felt like there was something off about that smile—it was as though you could count every one of Blue Moon's teeth. And some of them looked sharp. "Enjoy your visit with your friends! I'm off to walk Bram and Bela."

Every time she encountered the Moon sisters' odd parents, Scootaloo was glad she lived with Aunt Holiday and Auntie Lofty.

The fillies headed for the kitchen. But after opening drawers to find only cobwebs and peering into the refrigerator, which seemed to be housing some kind of mold experiment, they decided to move on to the greenhouse.

The air in the greenhouse was humid and heavy. Scootaloo almost felt as if she were swimming in a sea of plants.

"Show us where you went on the night of the slumber party," Apple Bloom prompted. Scootaloo tried to remember her exact path, but things looked very different in the daytime.

"I ran toward the back," she said, trotting deeper into the green glass enclosure. Her eye fell on a crooked ceramic pot. Now *that* she recognized. It matched the bruise on her forehead. "And I bumped into this!" She reached a hoof toward the soft feathery plant. Ambermoon quickly swatted it away.

"Don't touch that plant!" she said sharply. Scootaloo felt a knot form in her stomach. She already *had* touched it—two nights ago.

"Why?" she asked, hoping to sound breezy. "What would happen if I did?"

Ambermoon arched an eyebrow. "It's a fear fern," she explained.

Lilymoon nodded in recognition. "Oh yeah! I didn't know Dad was growing those."

"What do fear ferns do?" Sweetie Belle wondered. Scootaloo saw she was eyeing the plant as if it were a chimera ready to pounce.

"They give life to the thing that frightens you the most. But only you can see it," Ambermoon said grimly. "Sound familiar?"

"Okay, yes. I bumped into that plant and picked it up," Scootaloo admitted. "But I don't know why it made the Olden Pony show up. I'm totally over my fear of her! Mostly."

"That still doesn't explain why *we* can see the Olden Pony." Apple Bloom frowned. "We never touched the fern."

Ambermoon didn't have an answer for that.

"So now that we know what caused the problem, what's the cure?" Sweetie Belle wanted to know. Ambermoon and Lilymoon exchanged a worried look.

"There *isn't* one!" came a creaky voice from behind a cactus.

CHAPTER ELEVEN

The fillies whipped their heads toward the voice. It was Auntie Eclipse. *When did she come in the greenhouse?* Scootaloo wondered. Had she just been hiding there all along?

"That is, there isn't a cure unless you know me." Auntie Eclipse chuckled uproariously. Scootaloo laughed, too, though she wasn't sure what was so funny. She was just glad to know that there was a way to get rid of the Olden Pony.

"Follow me. Let's have some tea and a nice chat," Auntie Eclipse said, making her way out of the greenhouse.

Lilymoon and Ambermoon followed their aunt, and after a moment, the Crusaders did, too.

Auntie Eclipse led the young ponies to the library. It smelled like dust and age and books. Light filtered down through grimy windows and cobwebbed shelves, casting eerie spotlights. Scootaloo knew that Auntie Eclipse usually didn't let visitors into this place. But today, the strange, old pony seemed downright social!

Auntie Eclipse patted some moth-eaten cushions and invited the fillies to sit. Apple Bloom plopped down on one, and a huge puff of dust exploded from it. She sneezed loudly. Scootaloo decided to just stand.

"Get the tea tray, would you, dear?" Auntie Eclipse asked Ambermoon.

"Are you sure that's a good ide—" Lilymoon began, but Auntie Eclipse turned a sour eye on her niece, and she fell silent.

Ambermoon returned with a tray of strange small sandwiches and what appeared to be raisin cookies. Scootaloo watched as Sweetie Belle politely took one, and then dropped it in shock as the "raisins" moved.

"On second thought, we're not very hungry," Sweetie Belle said.

So much for trying to be polite, Scootaloo thought.

Auntie Eclipse poured tea for everypony, but none of them took a sip. "It's so nice you young ponies came to visit me." Auntie Eclipse smiled. It seemed to Scootaloo that she'd forgotten why they were all there in the first place.

"We're hoping you can tell us more about the fear fern. Why did it affect all of us when only Scootaloo touched it? And can you give us the cure?" Ambermoon gently prompted her aunt.

"Your father has been breeding especially strong fear ferns. Normally, they only work on the pony who touches them. But Blue Moon's ferns are contagious. This little Pegasus," Auntie Eclipse said, shaking an admonishing hoof at Scootaloo, "infected everypony she touched with her fear spores."

Scootaloo gasped. Not only was the Olden Pony's appearance her fault...she'd spread the problem to her friends, too.

"You said there was a cure," Lilymoon reminded Auntie Eclipse.

"So I did, so I did." The old pony nodded. "Got it off a traveling salespony from Saddle Arabia many moons ago."

She rummaged around in a weathered cabinet and pulled out a vial of blue liquid. Auntie Eclipse held it up to her eye and shook the bottle. Then she nodded. "Should be just enough for you five in here." Scootaloo's heart sank.

"You five?" she asked weakly. Auntie Eclipse turned her sharp gaze on Scootaloo.

"Well, yes. How many ponies did you touch, dear?" Scootaloo started to count.

"Um, both of my aunts. And Pinkie Pie and the Cakes when we were looking for Rainbow Dash. And Rainbow Dash…"

"And Rarity. Miss Cheerilee. Big McIntosh. Featherweight…. All the ponies in line at the market when we squeezed past them—" Ambermoon added.

"Don't forget the ponies on the train," Apple Bloom chimed in.

"And all the ponies we passed in the stands at the Canterlot Wonderbolts show. And the announcer," Sweetie Belle said, her eyes getting huge.

"So…a lot," Lilymoon finished. Auntie Eclipse clucked her tongue.

"Oh dear. That's bad. You see, if enough ponies believe in the same fear…it becomes a permanent part of our world. The same way a strong friendship can create magic. In this case, a shared fright feeds strength to whatever is feared. Your Olden Pony just went from being a foal's ghost story to a real problem."

Scootaloo plopped down on a cushion in defeat, ignoring the dust that plumed up around her. She'd unleashed a terror on Ponyville. Maybe even on Canterlot. And there was no way to stop it.

CHAPTER TWELVE

"You really think Twilight can help us?" Scootaloo asked for the seventh time. Lilymoon, Ambermoon, and the Crusaders were racing toward Princess Twilight Sparkle's castle. Even though she'd said the same thing the last six times, Sweetie Belle reassured Scootaloo.

"Twilight's saved Equestria more times than I can count! Besides, our sisters and their friends are the bravest ponies we know!"

A screaming streak of rainbow zoomed past them. Scootaloo paused, frowning in confusion. Was that...?

"Rainbow Dash?" she called.

The colorful blur did a three-point turn in midair and blazed back toward them. It was Rainbow Dash, and she looked terrified.

"Did you see her? Is she here?" Rainbow Dash asked, glancing around jerkily.

"Who?" asked Apple Bloom.

"The Olden Pony! She's terrorizing the town!" Rainbow Dash was freaking out. Scootaloo hated to see her idol so upset. Especially since *she* was the one responsible for passing the fear fern spores to Rainbow Dash. "Go ahead. Say it. I was wrong; you were right. The Olden Pony is real! And she keeps screaming for her rusty horseshoe. Why would anypony want a rusty horseshoe? It doesn't make any sense!" Rainbow Dash gestured wildly.

"Don't worry. We're on our way to get Princess Twilight. We think she can fix this," Scootaloo told her.

"What? But Twilight's in town. Where the Olden Pony is! You don't want to go there!" Rainbow Dash tried to drag Scootaloo in the opposite direction.

"We have…a…plan!" Ambermoon said, grabbing Scootaloo and trying to pull her back.

"Now, what in the deep-dish strudel is goin' on here?" Applejack's voice rang out. As she walked up, Fluttershy at her side, she tipped her hat back to squint at the odd scene. "Are y'all playin' tug-of-war with Scootaloo?"

Apple Bloom took a deep breath and tried to explain everything as fast as she could. "Scootaloo bumped into a fear fern at Lilymoon's house and now the Olden Pony is real and everypony who Scootaloo touched can see her and—"

Applejack stomped a hoof to interrupt her little sister. "Now, Apple Bloom. You know I only want the truth."

"We'll show them, won't we?" came a terrifyingly familiar voice. Rainbow Dash and the fillies jumped, startled to see the Olden Pony creep out from behind a stand of trees.

"Where'd she come from?" Sweetie Belle whimpered.

"Where'd *who* come from?" Fluttershy asked, looking quizzically from the cowering ponies to Applejack.

"The Olden Pony," Scootaloo said weakly. The spooky old mare looked different now—somehow more solid. Bigger. And much scarier. Auntie Eclipse was right, Scootaloo realized. The ponies' fear was making her stronger. The Olden Pony advanced on the group, muttering horribly under her breath. Scootaloo shrank back.

Fluttershy looked at her in concern. "Oh no. It sounds like you're seeing things. Maybe you're getting sick. Do you have a fever?" Fluttershy laid a cool hoof on Scootaloo's forehead before she could jerk away.

"Don't touch her!" the Crusaders and Moon sisters yelled.

Fluttershy leaped back, startled and hurt. "Why not?"

"*Because now you're mine, too,*" came a voice like the sound of creaking hinges.

Fluttershy's eyes grew wide and she backed away, trembling. *"It's the...the... Olden Pony!"*

Applejack frowned at Fluttershy, then

her expression cleared with a realization.

"Oh, I get it. This is one of your practical jokes, huh, Dash? Okay, I'll play. *Ooooh*. I'm so scared of the Golden Pony." Applejack pretended to be frightened.

"*Olden* Pony!" Rainbow Dash corrected her.

"Fine. Now. Aren't we supposed to be havin' a little chitchat with these fillies about their behavior at your Wonderbolts show?" Applejack asked. Neither Rainbow Dash nor Fluttershy answered. Their eyes were locked on the red Cyclops-like glare of the ancient mare. Applejack sighed. "Guess it's up to me, then. C'mon, y'all," she told the CMCs and their friends, shooing them forward with a hoof, "let's go." And then Applejack nudged Scootaloo.

Scootaloo watched miserably as Applejack finally saw what the others were reacting to. Her jaw dropped, and her eyes grew wide in terror. She backed up, next to Rainbow Dash and Fluttershy, quaking. Then all three of them stampeded away, the Olden Pony cackling in terrible pursuit.

"Listen," Ambermoon told the others, "remember what Auntie Eclipse said? Shared fear gives the Olden Pony more power. Maybe she'll go away if we can convince everypony in town not to be afraid."

"First we have to convince ourselves," Apple Bloom pointed out.

CHAPTER THIRTEEN

When the group of five fillies arrived in town and turned down Ponyville's main street in search of Twilight, Scootaloo knew that there was no chance of doing what Ambermoon had suggested.

The town was in chaos. Ponies screamed and ran in terror. The Olden Pony almost seemed to be everywhere! Scootaloo watched as the Olden Pony popped out of an apple cart to scare Big McIntosh. As he stampeded off, the spooky pony disappeared, only to reappear in an alleyway, startling Miss Cheerilee. She even chased Filthy Rich in circles around the town square.

"I'll give you as many bits as you

want," Filthy Rich whimpered, "just leave me alone!"

"I don't want bits. I want my rusty horseshoe!" the Olden Pony proclaimed. Filthy Rich leaped into an open pickle barrel and pulled the lid on top, trying to hide. But the Olden Pony just cackled and gave the barrel a shove, sending it (and Filthy Rich) rolling down the street. Ponies leaped out of the way of the sloshing, screaming barrel. The Crusaders, Lilymoon, and Ambermoon ducked behind a building to get away from the hysteria.

"Scootaloo. You never finished your story," Lilymoon said suddenly.

Scootaloo was confused. "What story?"

"The Olden Pony story. How does it end? What makes her go away?"

Scootaloo shrugged. "The story doesn't

really have an end," she said, shaking her head. "She's just always wandering Equestria, yelling for her rusty horseshoe."

"Why's she so upset, anyhow?" Apple Bloom wondered.

"Maybe she's lonely," Ambermoon said. The other ponies all turned to look at her. Ambermoon carefully didn't meet their eyes. "I mean…it's easy to be angry when you don't have any friends. Or you feel like nopony is listening to you." Scootaloo could tell Ambermoon was speaking from experience. She knew how that felt, too.

"Yeah, when you guys didn't believe me, and I thought I was losing you as friends, it was pretty much the worst feeling ever," Scootaloo admitted.

"You think that's how the Olden Pony

feels?" Sweetie Belle asked with wide eyes. "She just wants a friend?"

Scootaloo started to laugh at the very idea of it, but then she paused. Why not? Nopony ever actually talked to the Olden Pony. They just ran away from her. That did sound pretty lonely.

"I think I might have an idea of how to stop everypony from being afraid," said Scootaloo. "But I'm gonna need some help."

"What are friends for?" Apple Bloom grinned. "We're in!"

CHAPTER FOURTEEN

Everypony seems to be talking at once,
Scootaloo thought. Twilight and her
friends sat at their thrones around the map
table in the Castle of Friendship, arguing
and recounting their horrific experiences
with the Olden Pony. Lilymoon,
Ambermoon, and the Crusaders stood
nearby, waiting to get a word in edgewise.
Finally, Twilight Sparkle raised her hooves
to interrupt the cacophony.

"And the reason this ghost story became
real is because your father is growing
especially powerful fear ferns?" Twilight
asked, fixing her eyes on Ambermoon and
Lilymoon. Scootaloo squirmed for them.
She'd been in trouble enough times to

know how intense Twilight's gaze could be. "First the bogle, then the werepony, now this. I'm not sure I like how much dangerous magic seems to be coming from your family's house." Twilight frowned.

"It wasn't our father's plant. He's just… watching it for a friend," Lilymoon said quickly. Scootaloo blinked. Lilymoon was lying! It was just a small lie…but why? The other Crusaders glanced at Scootaloo. They'd noticed, too.

"Whatever the case, we need to stop this fear before it gets any stronger," Twilight said. She thought for a moment. "The Olden Pony keeps asking for her rusty horseshoe. Maybe we could try just giving her what she wants?" she suggested.

"I already tried that. It didn't work; she just knocked it aside and kept chasing us,"

Scootaloo explained. "But…I think I may have another idea." Twilight nodded for Scootaloo to continue. She felt a little nervous, laying out her plan to the bravest ponies in Equestria, but she cleared her throat and went for it. "We'll need everypony in town to help. Hopefully, that'll be enough to cover the ones I accidentally touched in Canterlot, too." Scootaloo looked around the room as she explained. "Spooky things aren't as scary when you understand them. And I think the Olden Pony just needs understanding and friendship." The others looked at her, waiting for her to go on. "So I thought we could all welcome her as our new friend," Scootaloo finished lamely.

"That's it? *That's* your plan?" Rainbow Dash asked in disbelief.

"It does seem rather simplistic," Rarity chimed in. And suddenly, all the ponies were talking over one another again.

"*Hey!*" Sweetie Belle yelled. The older ponies fell silent. Scootaloo was just as shocked as they were. She hadn't known such a loud noise could come out of Sweetie Belle. "You didn't believe us when we tried to tell you about the Timberwolf, either. Well, this time, you'd better listen! Or we'll all be in even worse trouble! I mean…uh…please," Sweetie Belle added politely.

"Sweetie Belle has a point," Twilight said dryly. "We did promise to listen to you fillies in the future. And I agree that friendship is stronger than fear. What do you need from us, Scootaloo?"

CHAPTER FIFTEEN

The tiniest hoofshaving of moon hung in the sky above the Ponyville town square. Scootaloo stood alone in the eerie darkness, shivering. She was beginning to rethink her plan. But it was a little late for that. She stepped bravely forward and yelled into the night.

"OLDEN PONY! I WANT TO TALK TO YOU!"

A freezing wind, colder than Scootaloo had ever felt, blew past. Icicles formed on the nearby eaves, and a chill danced down Scootaloo's back.

"Whoooo calls?" The Olden Pony's voice creaked, echoing from all corners of the town. The shadows cast by the shops

seemed to grow and mass together before revealing a huge figure with a single glowing flame of an eye. Scootaloo gulped. Fear had definitely made the ancient mare stronger. She tried to keep her voice steady as she answered.

"I do. Scootaloo. I hear you're looking for something."

"MY RUSTY HORSESHOE! WHERE IS IT? WHERRRRRRREEEE?" In the blink of an eye, the Olden Pony was towering over Scootaloo, her dark shawl seeming to blot out even the light of the stars.

"I already gave you one of those and you didn't want it," Scootaloo said, bravely holding her ground. "I think you're really looking for something else."

"WHAT?" the Olden Pony demanded, leering at Scootaloo.

"Friendship," Scootaloo said, forcing a smile despite her fear.

The Olden Pony hesitated. She seemed to be considering that. Scootaloo quickly continued, pressing her advantage. "I think nopony ever listens to you, so I will. That's what it means to be a friend. Tell me about your rusty horseshoe. Why do you want it so badly?"

The Olden Pony appeared confused. Scootaloo realized that this must be the first time the ancient mare hadn't had a pony run away from her. Maybe she wasn't sure what to do.

"I...*need it?*" the Olden Pony said, hesitantly raising the hoof without a shoe.

"Why does it have to be rusty?" Scootaloo asked. Her constant questions seemed to be keeping the Olden Pony from pouncing on her. Plus, she *had* always wondered about that.

"I'm not sure." The Olden Pony seemed to consider this, surprised.

"Then why don't you let your new friends give you something nicer?" Scootaloo suggested. She flared her wings wide and yelled, *"Now!"*

The doors of every building in the town square suddenly swung open, and the residents of Ponyville poured out. Scootaloo could see they looked nervous, but her friends led them forward. Everypony held something in their forehoof—each object the same yet different. The Olden Pony looked at them, then glared.

"WHERE'S MY RUSSSSSSTY HORSESHOOOOOEEEE?" she rasped menacingly.

"Try this on instead," Apple Bloom said, moving to stand alongside Scootaloo. She held out a candy-apple-red horseshoe for the Olden Pony. The ancient mare frowned and leaned down to examine it. "I painted it special for you, my new friend!"

"You can have this one, too," Sweetie Belle squeaked, joining Scootaloo's other side and trying not to tremble as she held out a soft embroidered horseshoe. "My sister helped me design it for you."

"And these are from us," Ambermoon said. She and Lilymoon held out horseshoes that were perfect opposites, like the sisters themselves. One shoe was white with a black stripe; the other was black with a white stripe.

"I...I...*don't understand,*" the Olden Pony said, sounding unsure for the first time. *"You should be running from me!"*

"We don't run from our friends, silly!" Rainbow Dash said, flying up with a Wonderbolt-blue horseshoe in her hooves. It even had tiny lightning bolts decorating it, Scootaloo noticed.

One by one, the other ponies stepped forward to present their gifts to the surprised Olden Pony. Soon horseshoes of every shape, size, color, and material formed a pile in front of the ancient mare. Shiny shoes, polka-dot shoes, ribbon-wound shoes, flowery shoes, shoes that made music when you stepped on them. Cranky Doodle's shoe was made of an old toupee. And Pinkie Pie had baked a cupcake in the shape of a horseshoe.

"For when you get hungry on a walk," she explained brightly.

The Olden Pony just stood there, staring at the mountain of horseshoes. She looked around at the sea of smiling pony faces surrounding her.

"You're…not afraid?" the Olden Pony asked.

And then Scootaloo knew what she had to do. She didn't like it. But she was the only pony who could do it.

"Nope. We're just glad you're our friend," she said. And then she leaned close to the terrifying mare and hugged her. The Olden Pony froze…then patted Scootaloo's back with her unshod hoof.

"Well. Thank you, dearie," the Olden Pony said. And then…she disappeared, along with the pile of horseshoes.

The town square erupted in cheers!

"Yaaaay, Scootaloo! You did it! She's

gone! We're saved!" Ponies surrounded Scootaloo and hoisted her onto their shoulders. Scootaloo grinned, although she couldn't help but feel a little pang of guilt—after all, if she hadn't infected the ponies with the fear fern in the first place, none of this would've happened. Apple Bloom seemed to guess what she was thinking, and she beamed up at her friend.

"Just go with it!" she said.

CHAPTER SIXTEEN

The next morning, everypony worked together to clean up the chaos in the town from the terror of the day before. By noon, it was as though the Olden Pony had never been there.

"That's the power of friendship in action," Applejack said, admiring the sparkling town square. *And good soap,* Scootaloo thought, smiling to herself.

The Crusaders, Lilymoon, and Ambermoon joined Twilight and her friends at Sugarcube Corner for a well-deserved treat after their cleaning spree. Pinkie Pie trotted out with more of the horseshoe cupcakes she had baked, but the fillies declined to try them.

"Uh…too soon," Scootaloo explained to Pinkie.

"More for me!" Pinkie Pie shrugged and happily nommed the cakes herself.

"Hey…" Rainbow Dash pulled Scootaloo aside with a wing. "I just wanted to say I'm sorry for giving you a hard time about the Olden Pony. Just 'cause I didn't see her doesn't mean I shouldn't have listened to you. We okay?"

"Totally," Scootaloo said, relieved that things were right with Rainbow Dash again.

"And before I forget, these are for you," Rainbow Dash said, holding out five tickets with the Wonderbolts logo on them. "VIP tickets for you and your friends to our Cloudsdale Expo. It's about twenty percent cooler than the Flyfest," she added with a wink.

"Really?" Scootaloo couldn't believe it. "You sure you want us there after last time?"

"Just try not to shut down *this* show." Rainbow Dash smiled, giving Scootaloo's head a playful noogie.

As the other ponies finished up their treats, Twilight Sparkle addressed the group.

"There have been a lot of strange things happening in Ponyville lately. And while we've managed to handle all of them before they got too out of hoof, I'm worried about what will come next." Twilight turned to the Unicorn sisters. "Lilymoon, Ambermoon. I think it's time my friends and I had a talk with your family. I have quite a few questions about the safety of the magic they're practicing."

Lilymoon and Ambermoon shared a worried look.

"Our family is pretty private," Lilymoon said at the same time as Ambermoon spoke: "I don't think that's such a good idea." Scootaloo was pretty sure it was the first time she'd seen the sisters agree on something. They must have really not wanted Twilight to visit the house on Horseshoe Hill. But Twilight persisted.

"I know it might be an uncomfortable conversation," Twilight said. "But it's necessary. I don't want any more dangerous surprises in our town. Now, if you'll please lead us to your parents?"

Lilymoon and Ambermoon hung their heads. But they nodded and started out of Sugarcube Corner, Twilight and her friends following.

"I hope we didn't get them into trouble," Sweetie Belle worried when they were gone. Scootaloo nodded. The Moon family wasn't the most understanding bunch of ponies.

"Especially since we just made friends with Ambermoon," Apple Bloom added. "You were right, Scootaloo. She's nice!"

"And brave," Sweetie Belle agreed.

"Yeah, both sisters are," Scootaloo said. But something was still bothering her. "Do you think we can trust them? I mean, I can't imagine either of them wanting to turn anypony into a Timberwolf."

"But if they didn't…then who did?" Apple Bloom wondered.

"And why did Lilymoon lie to Twilight about the fear fern?" Sweetie Belle asked.

None of them had any answers. And Scootaloo was sure that if they didn't find out what was going on soon, life in Ponyville would get even weirder *and* more dangerous. She looked at her two best friends and smiled. No matter what mysteries were hiding on Horseshoe Hill, she knew that as long as she had the two of them by her side, the Cutie Mark Crusaders could handle *any*thing that came their way. At least…she hoped so.

EPILOGUE

The Pony was intrigued. As annoying as those Cutie Mark Crusaders were, this time, they had actually been helpful. The Pony hadn't realized a fear fern could be so powerful. It would work nicely with The Pony's plan. The Princess of Friendship may be sticking her muzzle where it didn't belong, but soon it would be too late for her to do anything. Things were starting to fall into place. The Pony would enter the Livewood. And then, the real fun would start.